written by
Jo Dodd

illustrated by
Jenifer Novak Landers

Tilly Toad's
HEAVY LOAD

Copyright 2021 by Jo Dodd

Illustrations by Jenifer Novak Landers

All rights reserved. Permission to reproduce any selection from this book

must be granted in writing from the author. This book is produced by

Fully Inspired Publishing. www.fullyinspiredpublishing.com

The text of this book is set in Papyrus.

The illustrations are mixed media and computer illustration.

Library of Congress Catalogue-in-Publication Data is on file.

ISBN 978-1-7366082-1-0

For Terence, Deon, Drew,
Ethan and Joseph.

Your love and support is
all I need to be brave
in this world.

In loving memory of
Edward Pinkney Hopps,
a beloved father
and grandfather
whose legacy brings
love and laughter
for generations to come.
~Jo

For my daughter Stella
who shows the world
what it looks like to
believe in yourself.
~Jenifer

It was a beautiful day on Lilyflower Pond.

In a little cottage, by the banks of the pond, Tilly Toad groaned as his Mum cheerfully called upstairs.

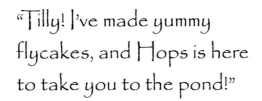

"Tilly! I've made yummy flycakes, and Hops is here to take you to the pond!"

"UGH!" groaned Tilly.

"I don't want flycakes, and I definitely don't want to go to the pond with Hops!"

Tilly was worrying about starting school the next day
at Lilyflower Academy.

Usually he loved spending time with Hops but on this day,
he just wanted to stay in bed.

All Tilly could think about was what would happen the next day at school.

He was nervous, worried and afraid that the other frogs and toads would laugh at him.

Tilly crawled slowly
into the kitchen
where a cheerful Hops
was ready to go.

"Come on little toad,
today will be TOADTilly amazing!"

"Ugh!" sighed Tilly. "I'm not so sure about that....."
"......Hops wait! You're going too fast!"

When Tilly caught up with Hops, his heart sank.
He had a feeling his grandfather was up to something strange.

"Tell me Tilly,
what's bothering you today?"
asked Hops as he placed a stone
in Tilly's backpack.

"Ugh!" sighed Tilly.
"I'm scared about school.
What if they laugh at my spots?"

Hops studied another stone.

With a curious smile he
wrote something on it,
and placed it in the backpack.

"I'm nervous," continued Tilly.
"What if they laugh at my name?"
"....and what if I don't fit in?"

"Hops, stop! Why are you putting stones in my backpack?"

"Why do you think they will laugh?" asked Hops,
ignoring Tilly's question as he picked up yet another stone.

"They'll laugh because I'm different,"
cried Tilly. "No one looks like me, and
no one has a name like mine....."

"Oh, you're *different*......" muttered
Hops, while placing another stone in
the backpack.

"....Hmmmm, right.... I think we're done here now.
Let's go Toady-O!" he sang and bounced down the path.

"Hops pleeeease help me!" cried Tilly.
"This backpack is too heavy!"

Hops stopped and turned with a sparkling glint in his eye.
He took the backpack from his grandson's shoulders and smiled.

"My goodness, you're right, Tilly!
This backpack *does* feel heavy."

"Let me help you little toad!"

Hops took the stones
from the backpack
and gave one to
his grandson.

"Tilly, hold this stone and tell me, is this you?
Are you a stone?"

"Nooooo" said Tilly, thinking that his grandfather
might have completely lost his mind!

"Oh thank goodness!" laughed Hops.
"Now, hold the stone
and tell me how it feels."

Tilly thought for a moment. "It feels heavy and cold."
"Great!" said Hops with delight.

"Now tell me Tilly, do you want to keep holding that stone, or do you want to throw it away?"

"Well, it doesn't feel good," said Tilly, "So I guess I'll throw it away."

"Then do it, little toad" laughed Hops.
"Take that heavy, cold stone
and think about how good it feels
to throw it away!"

Tilly threw the stone as hard
as he could into the pond.
It flew through the air
and made a huge
splash as it hit
the water.

STONE

Lilyflower
Pond

"Now Tilly," said Hops, picking up the next stone,
"you told me you were scared, but remember you could *feel* the
stone, **but you are not a stone, right?**"

"Yes, that's right" said Tilly.
"So, little toad, are you scared or do you just *feel* scared?"

Tilly held the stone. It felt cold and heavy like the other one.

Suddenly he knew what Hops was teaching him.

"I *feel* scared!" he said with excitement.

"I'm not scared, I just feel scared. I can take that feeling and throw it in the pond!

I get it Hops! I get it!"

"Hallelujah, he gets it!" laughed Hops.

"Now, let's do the same with the other stones!"

One by one,
Tilly held each stone
and thought about each feeling.

He threw the stones with all of his might into the pond. The last one nearly hit Mrs. Daphne Duck who was teaching her precious ducklings how to swim!

Tilly stood frozen in place, worrying that he was in trouble, but Hops was laughing so hard he could barely speak!

"Oh Tilly, that was TOADTilly terrific!

Now *there's* a tale we can tell many years from now!"

Tilly looked up at his grandfather with admiration. "Hops,
I don't know what I would do without you."

"Always remember this little toad" said Hops
"YOU have the power to change your thoughts!"

You have the power
to change your thoughts.

"Now come Tilly Billy"
sang the glorious
deep voice.

"We'd better get
a shakin',
there are stories
in the makin'!"

Tilly breathed in the warm summer air and smiled,
knowing that his first day at Lilyflower Academy
wouldn't be so bad after all.

Connect with Tilly!

We would love to hear from you.

www.TillyToad.com

Join us on Social Media. Links on the website. Hashtags #tillytoad, #toadtillyamazing, #teachtilly

Illustrator's Notes:

I felt an immediate connection to the characters of Tilly and Hops and knew this project would be life changing. A great rhythm of collaborating with Jo was filled with synchronicities from the start. Everything clicked along the way. I felt my artist soul was already aligned with bringing Tilly's world to life and I am deeply grateful for this project, which has been more about ALLOWING the work to come through rather than anything that feels like effort. Simply magical and meant to be!

Author's Notes:

As a Mum to four biracial young men, I have a passion to help children navigate their emotions around being 'different'. Tilly's stories tap into our universal desire for love, acceptance and belonging. My hope is that Tilly's tales will help us all recognize and celebrate our differences. I hold a vision that Tilly will be as beloved as Winnie the Pooh, bringing heartwarming stories and life lessons for generations to come. Jenifer and I were destined to meet; our 'Tilly' journey has been magical from the very beginning. One day, I'll write the "tale we can tell many years from now!"

Made in United States
Orlando, FL
02 September 2022

21910786R00020